BROKEND

_hydrus

Published by: Hydrus
Photography & Illustrated Art by: Hydrus
Cover Design by: Cleo Moran - Devoted Pages Designs
Formatting by: Cleo Moran - Devoted Pages Designs
https://www.devotedpages.com
Proofreading: Amina Jojo Dahmouche

Manufactured in the United States of America

The Library of Congress Cataloging-in-Publication Data is available upon request.

Paperback ISBN: 979-8-9856109-6-3
E-Book ISBN: 979-8-9856109-7-0

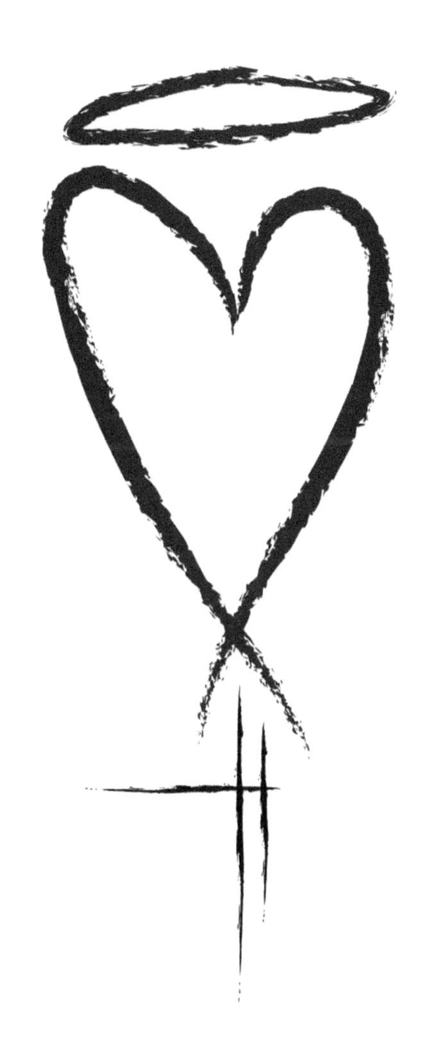

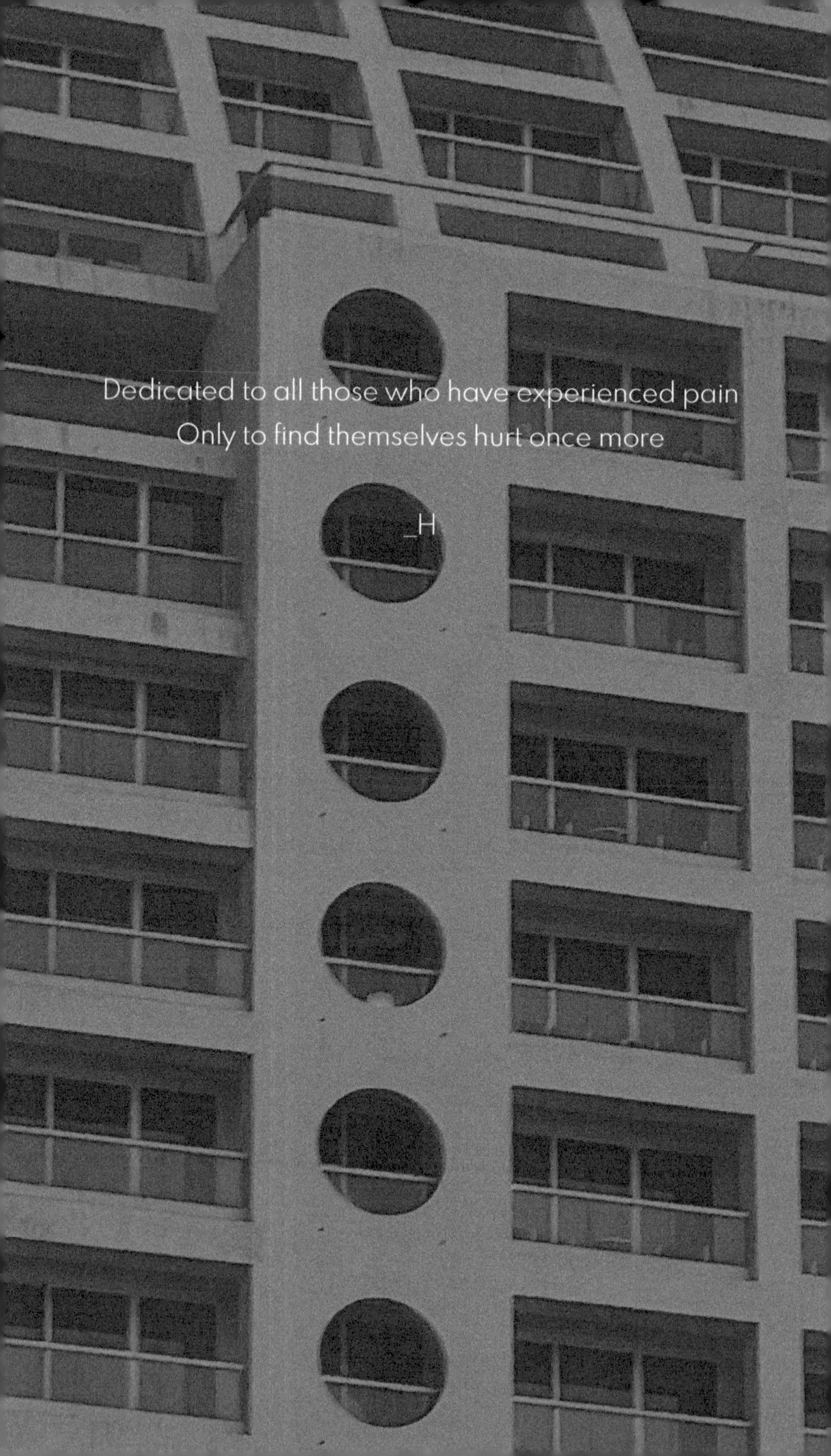
Dedicated to all those who have experienced pain
Only to find themselves hurt once more

_H

BrokEND

Welcome to the second book in the FallEND series.

In BrokEND, we embark on a journey to uncover the fate of Christian Black following his accident. We delve into the aftermath of his betrayal by someone he believed was his true love.

As the story unravels, we will delve into Christian's newfound path and the profound revelations that await his heart. Alongside him, he will find his bartender friend, Angeline, whose loyalty becomes increasingly significant in his journey to healing.

However, amidst it all, we remain vigilant, for Blair may still be lurking in the shadows, patiently waiting for another opportunity to capture Christian's heart.

So we find ourselves asking...

Will he ever be able to recover?

Will he be able to find redemption or have a chance at finding true love again?

Or will life just continue to ruin his hopes of finding true happiness.

Sometimes the universe speaks to us in waves, only to watch us drown in its infinite choir of noise.

_hydrus

ONE WAY
DO NOT
ENTER
DO NOT
ENTER
NO
BIKES PEDESTRIANS
SKATEBOARDS CARS

PEDESTRIANS
CYCLISTS
SKATERS
BUSES ONLY
We are broken just to be reopened   _hydrus

In disbelief
He barely breathes
His heart went silent
As no one grieves

How could it be
What shall I do
So many questions
There is no truth

Why Me
_hydrus

I was too high to remember I fell   _hydrus

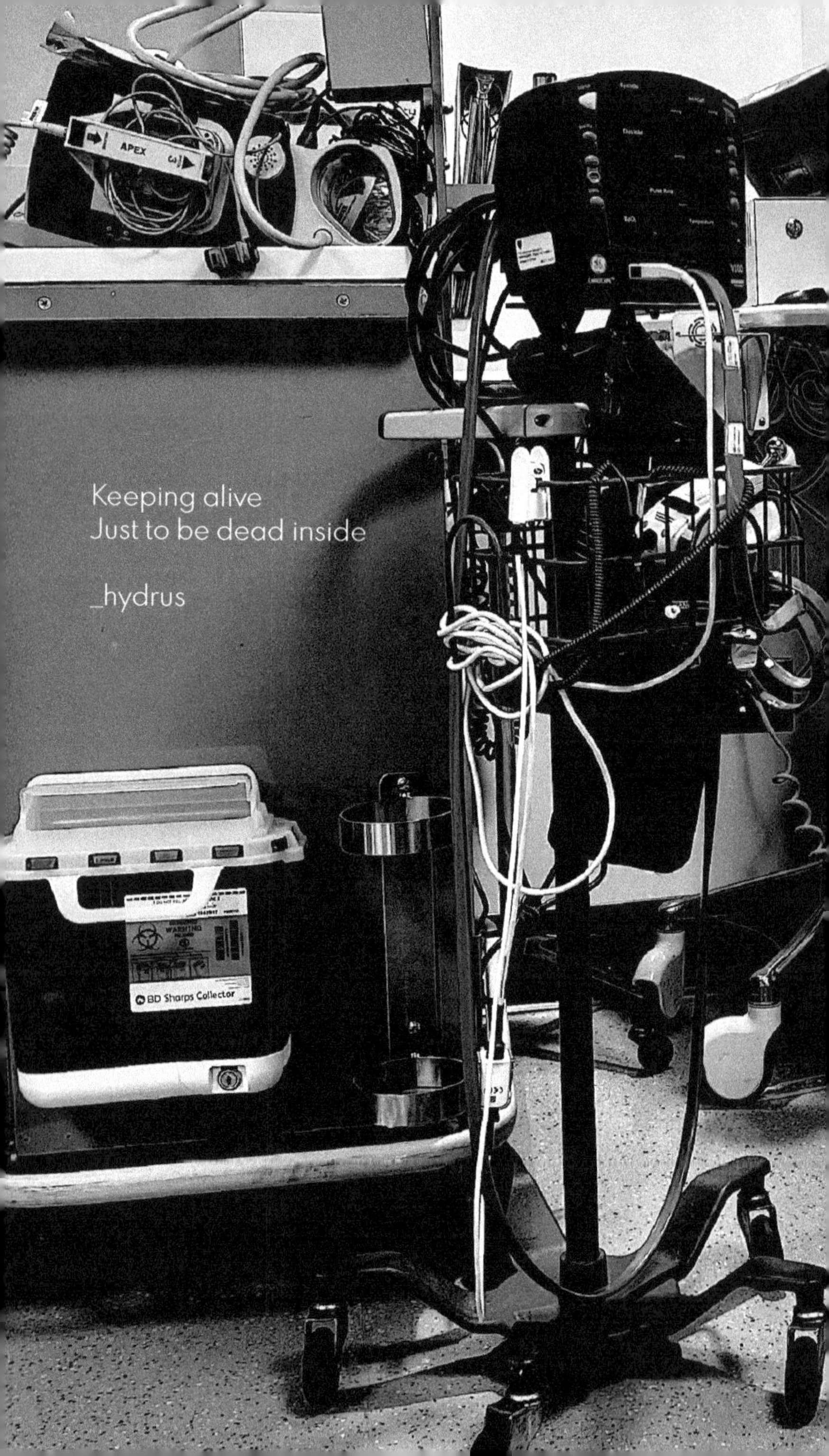

Keeping alive
Just to be dead inside

_hydrus

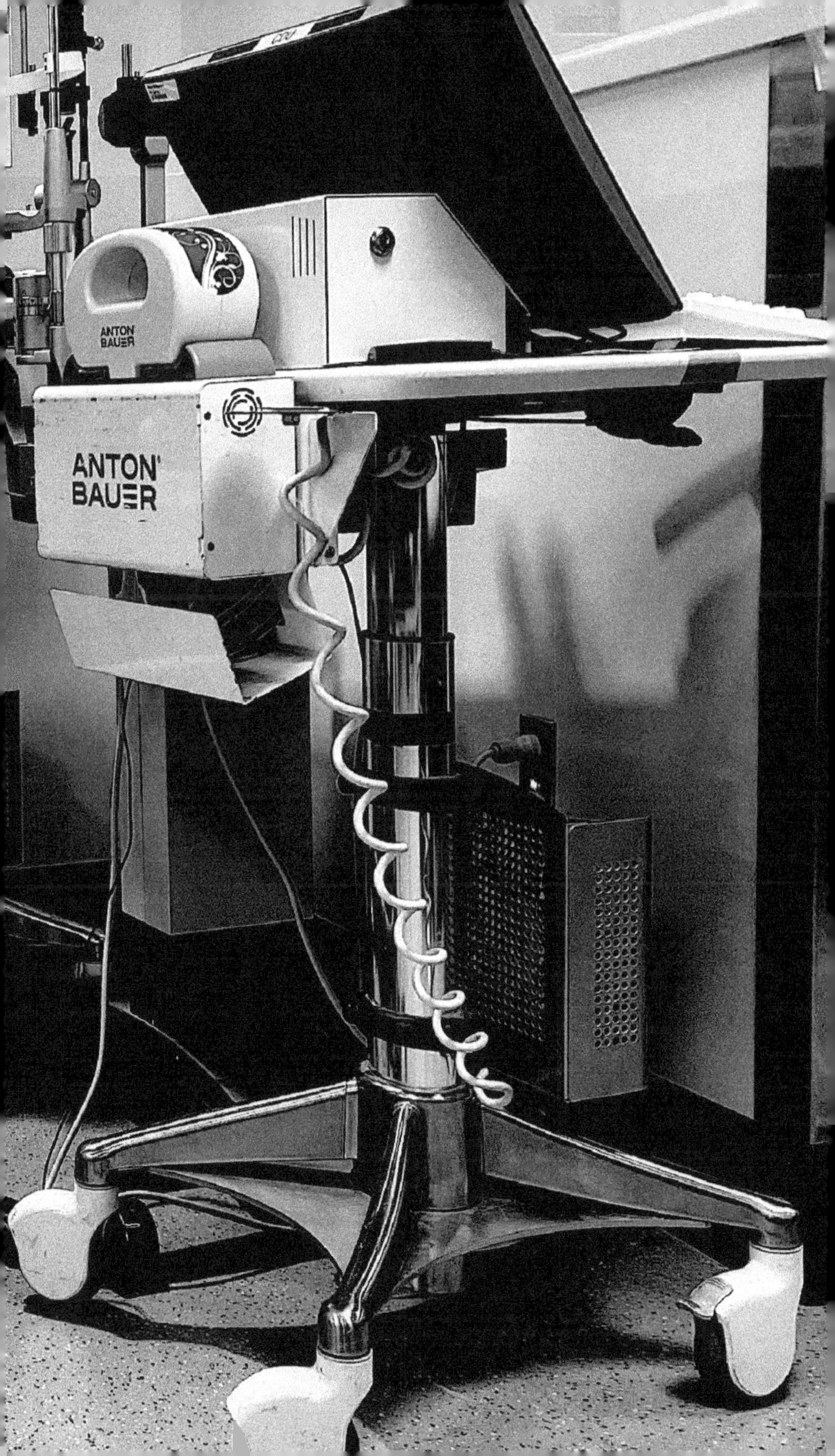

CPU
ANTON
BAUER
ANTON'
BAUER

There he lays
In somber sleep
Ripped apart
My eyes they weep

My gentle soul
It now commands
Fate led me here
Life's new demands

Purpose
_hydrus

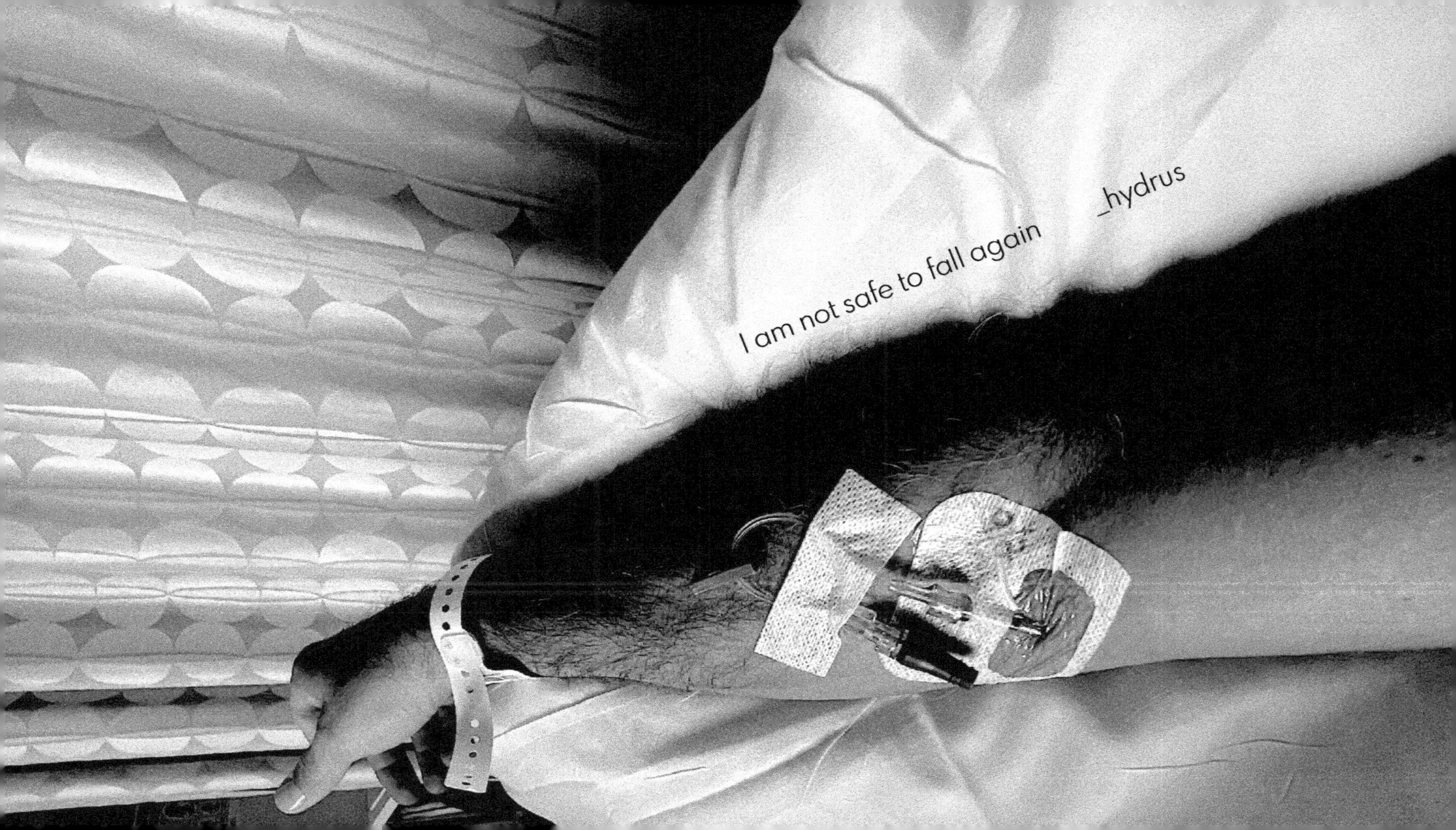

I am not safe to fall again   _hydrus

Early morning
The sun awakes
Eyes are dim
Mind contemplates

Is it a dream
Why am I here
Need to leave
Just disappear

At that moment
There is a beep
Sudden motions
A rescued sleep

Feeling a touch
His barren hand
The grip was tight
I quickly stand

Reached
_hydrus

Doors fly open
Nurses shout
Blood ignites
Many doubts

One reaches over
To check all signs
Heavens closed
Bless the divine

Life hasn't left
Light comes back
The veins react
As lungs contract

His solemn sleep
Has ended now
Lucks his guardian
I don't know how

Second Chance
_hydrus

Only fate can revive a broken heart _hydrus

They catch my sight
As questions blare
I'm not his wife
They talk and stare

Who can you be
We need to know
There is no mention
Of where he goes

I found your wings
Next to his chest
Grateful he has you
He needs to rest

John & Jane Doe
_hydrus

Emptiness holds hands with my grief   _hydrus

There was a note
A scribbled mess
Numbers were drawn
That was my guess

I now remember
One rainy night
Drinks were empty
Turned off the lights

We had been chatting
It was long ago
Still familiar
When you simply know

It was my napkin
The ink was blue
Across the phoenix
That's where he drew

Call Me
_hydrus

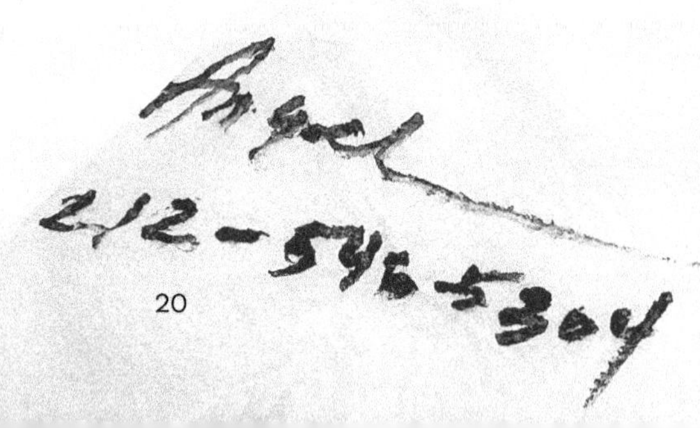

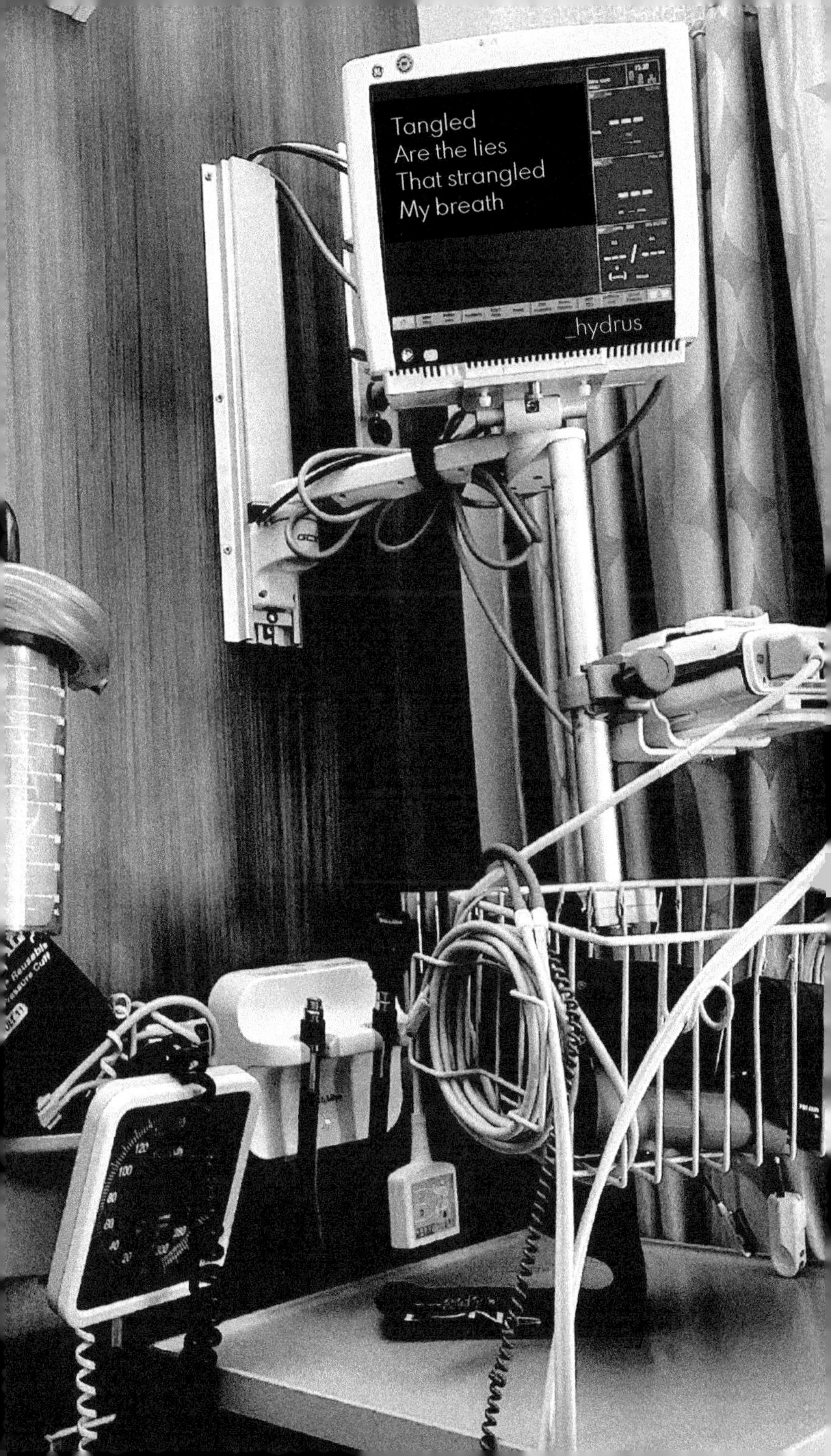

Tangled
Are the lies
That strangled
My breath
_hydrus

Glare is blinding
The body sore
Barely moving
Can't touch the floor

My mind is spinning
Images I dreamt
Mouth cannot speak
So sore and spent

Quickly glancing
She sleeps and waits
It feels familiar
So I hesitate

Why are we here
Confusion grows
Need some answers
Just don't know

Eyes get heavy
Light slowly dims
I return to slumber
To watch her swim

Dreaming
_hydrus

Staring at the clock
Hands drag in space
Minutes seem endless
I retrace her face

Those subtle lips
That pensive brow
It's night she sleeps
She knows me how

Clouded thoughts
Searching the maze
My minds entangled
Some things erased

But in this moment
The smoke goes clear
Her eyes are open
Our connections real

Remembered
_hydrus

i was made into a ghost just to witness me pass   _hydrus

Here she was
Her spirit heals
The ones she poured
The ones I feel

Fate brought us together
So I could fight
Faith cleansed my fear
My new found light

Grace
_hydrus

Moons have past
I get to heal
Time seems far
From the bended steel

But every day
She came to see
Be at my side
Right next to me

Many memories
Shared from our past
Remembered us
So many laughs

She was my angel
Who held my hand
Gathered my ashes
Would understand

Poured me drinks
Dealt with tales
When I was helpless
She did not fail

Here she was
Again in sight
Another chance
To ignite my light

Angeline
_hydrus

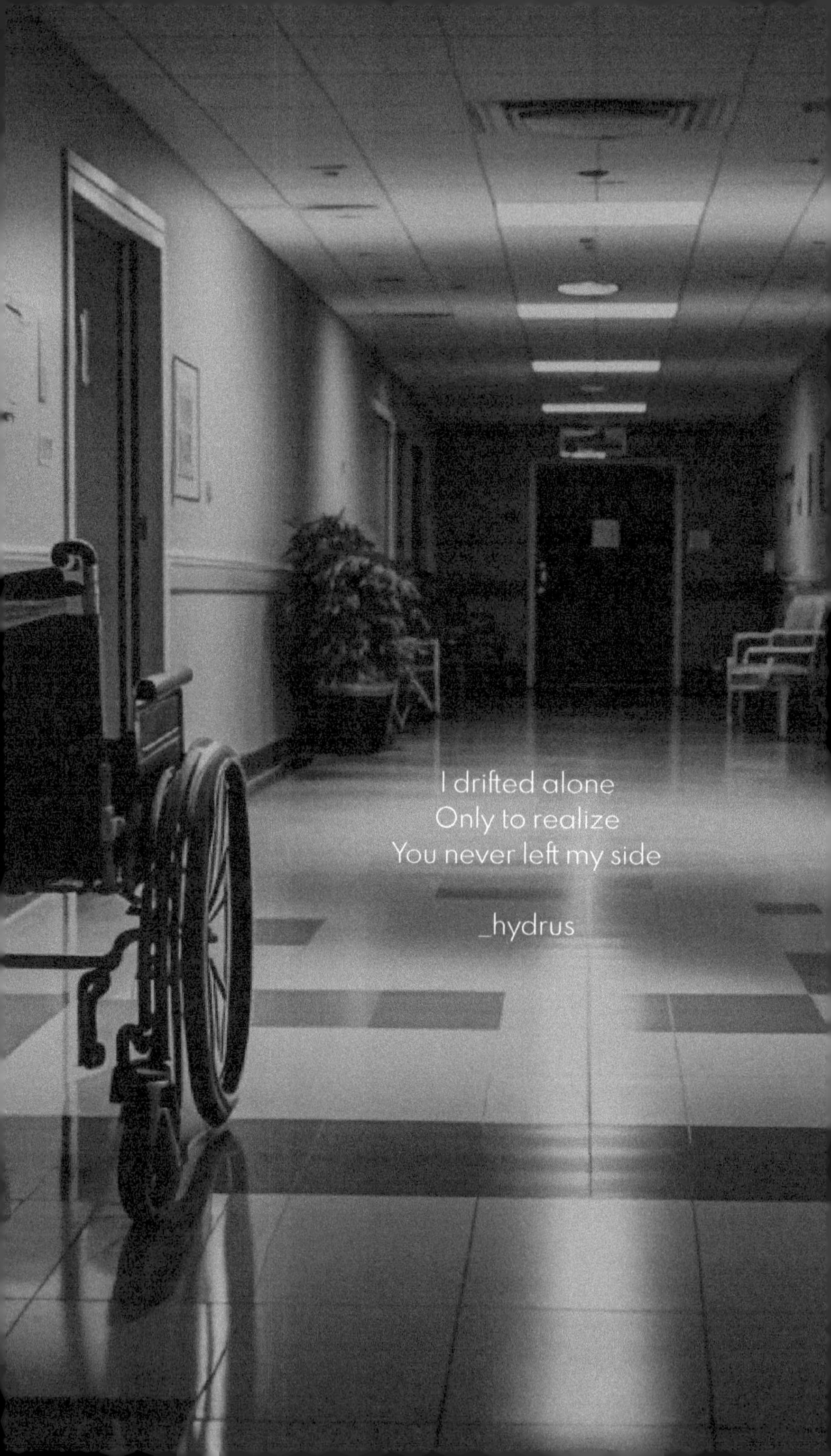

I drifted alone
Only to realize
You never left my side

_hydrus

A new sun rises
Sparks the sky
The nightmare's over
Where I almost died

The moments here
I now can go
Return to normal
To a vacant show

They rolled me out
She held my hand
We must depart
As I stand

The world awaits
Beyond just me
Let's keep in touch
My begging plea

She pecked my cheek
Lips graze my beard
Will I see you soon
You just need to heal

Farewell
_hydrus

Every step is a new abyss   _hydrus

STATE
LAW
STOP
FOR

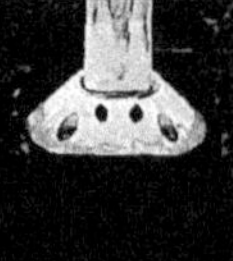
WITHIN
CROSSWALK

Still feeling bended
The days are tough
Wounds have mended
Life's still so rough

I'm still so haunted
By that crazy night
The day love ended
I'd taken flight

She was so cruel
As I fell again
Once more the fool
I can't pretend

My heart was trampled
I have the scars
Some from falling
Others she carved

Ruthless
_hydrus

Only the deepest depths can bring you light _hydrus

A new found journey
Struggles await
This mangled patient
Will enjoy his fate

Moving on
To eclipse my hell
Find myself
Amongst the shells

The barren city
Had plagued my heart
So many endings
Just need a start

Rebuild
_hydrus

I escaped the waves to drown in hers ..... hydrus

Endless horizons
With timeless skies
Sun filled valleys
Where wings can fly

A sandy quarter
I will call my home
Amongst the tide
To be left alone

CRANDON PARK
5
B

Not a moment
Just passes by
Relived the instant
When I almost died

Part of me
Has ended there
So much betrayal
Unlocked despair

In that darkness
Remained a light
It found her way
Returned my sight

Became the anchor
To my storm
She held the answers
I was reborn

Missing
_hydrus

It takes one moment to eclipse the rest
hydrus

All I do
Is think of her
A blinding smile
That fills my world

She nursed me back
To who I am
Then left my side
I could not stand

We stayed connected
It's not enough
The days feel endless
Missing her touch

Still the thoughts
Of a blurry past
When I found love
That didn't last

Flashes
_hydrus

I drink poison to feel alive   _hydrus

The sun continues
To rise and fall
And on each day
We always call

Timeless hours
For our souls to play
In her words
I get away

Distance far
Yet feelings near
She warms the heart
And keeps me clear

No more illusions
Or troubled ways
I want her close
Want her to stay

Languished
_hydrus

With every sip we fade away   _hydrus

I call her number
And hear her voice
Must ask her up
She has no choice

Take a flight
Come be with me
Need your touch
I'm so ready

Reaching Out
_hydrus

We both need answers no one can ask   _hydrus

Heart beats fast
I cannot wait
He wants me there
A true first date

So many times
Dreaming of this
His full attention
Maybe we kiss

Anticipation
_hydrus

Outside the clouds
Seem so vast
Heart quickly beats
See him at last

He spared no time
To get me there
His words were few
My thoughts are clear

I cannot wait
Time stands still
A long distance date
Restrained the thrill

Pulling the buckle
That straps me in
Dreams begin
Of impending sin

Descending
_hydrus

I blindly see what the heart follows   _hydrus

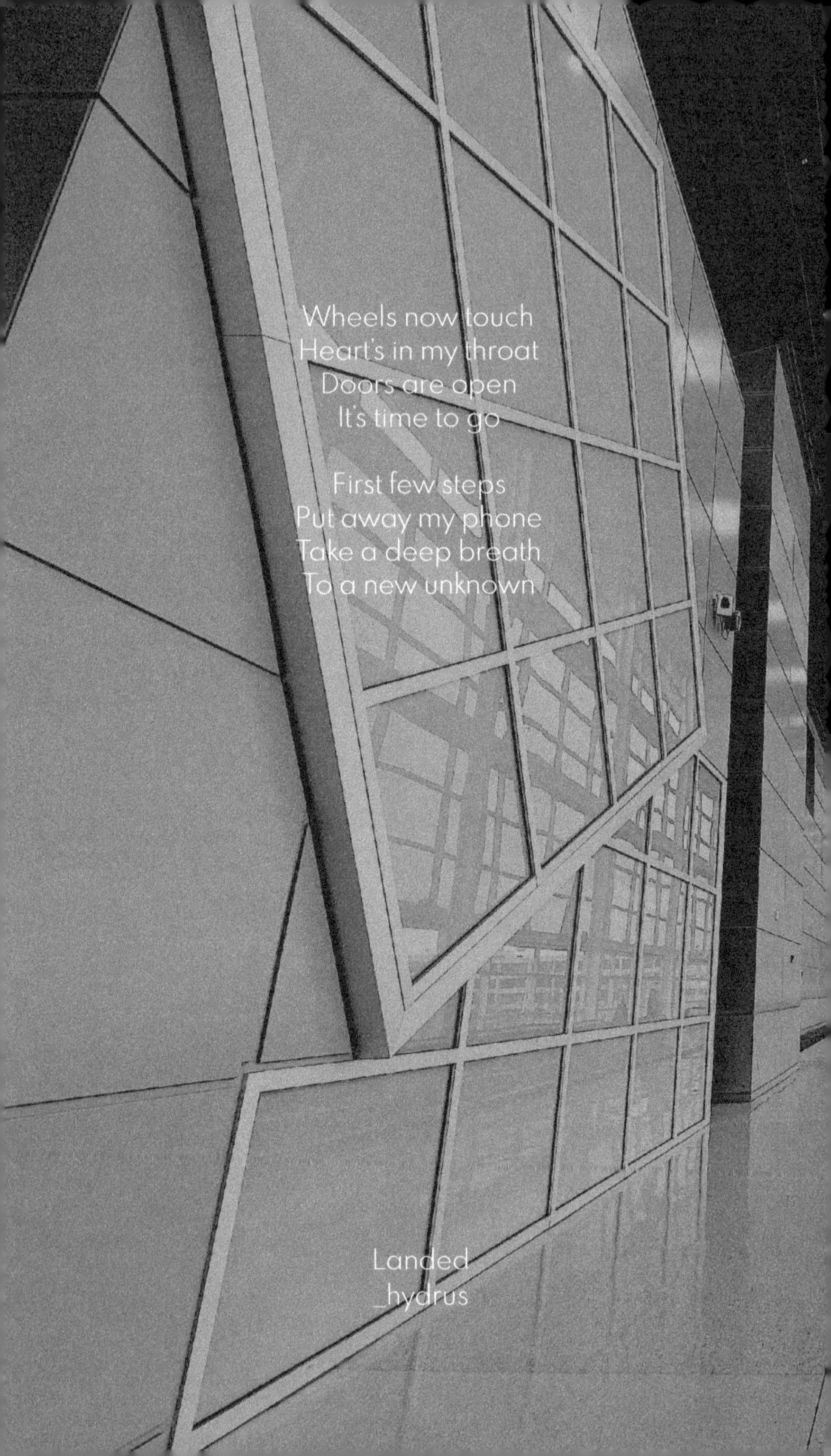

Wheels now touch
Heart's in my throat
Doors are open
It's time to go

First few steps
Put away my phone
Take a deep breath
To a new unknown

Landed
_hydrus

Tonight is special
Stars paint the sky
My angel returns
To be by my side

Plans are simple
Need her so much
My heart is hurting
Searching that touch

I can't explain it
Thoughts so blurred
Time has plagued me
Looking for words

The nerves are foolish
Feel like a child
Her flight arrived
I see her smile

Hello Again
_hydrus

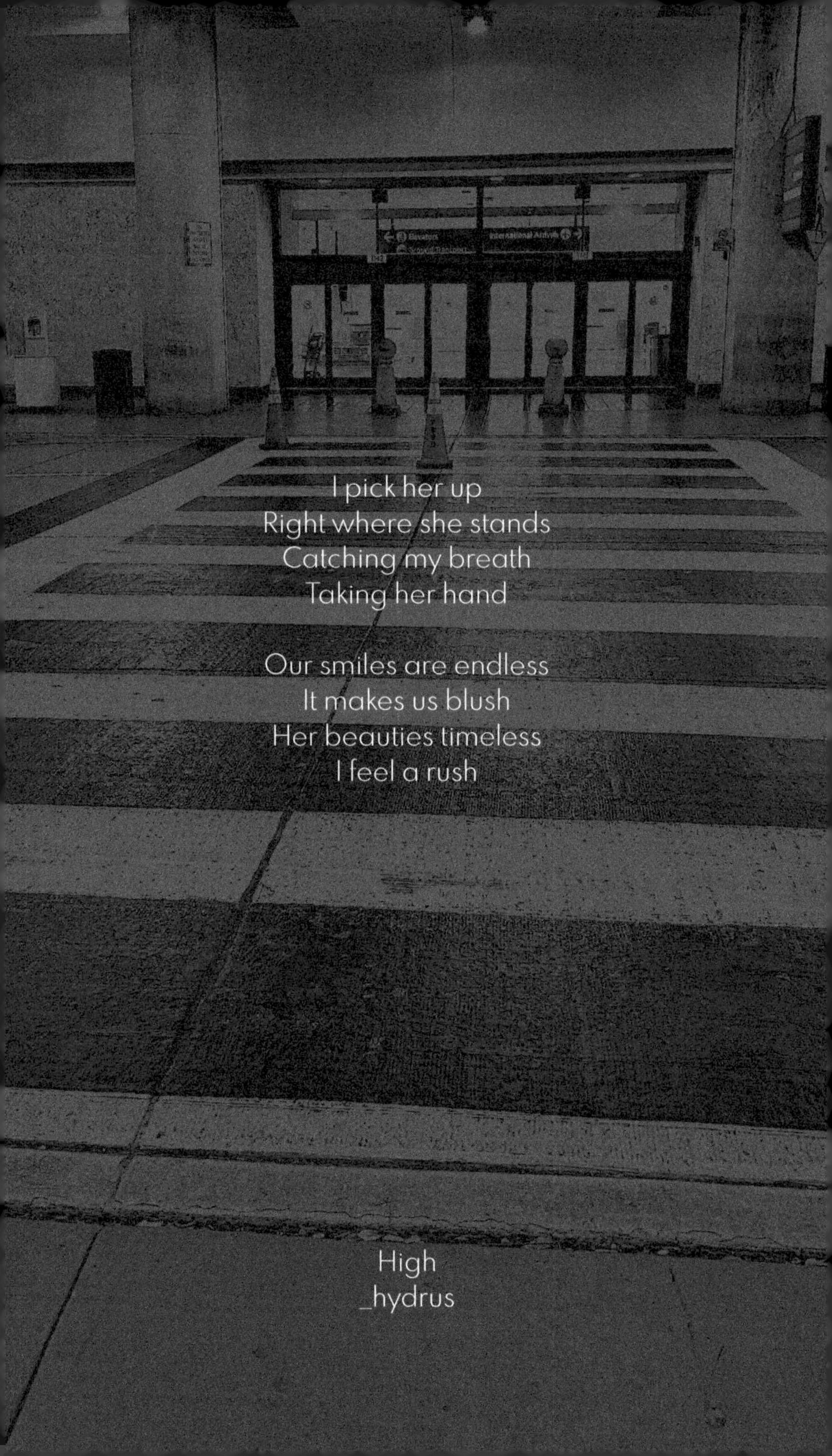

I pick her up
Right where she stands
Catching my breath
Taking her hand

Our smiles are endless
It makes us blush
Her beauties timeless
I feel a rush

High
_hydrus

I tell my driver
To take her things
And sit beside her
As her phone rings

She takes the call
From the hotel
It's from her boss
Who I know well

Words are muffled
Then it's done
Work is finished
Our time has come

I don't ask questions
Happy she's here
No more distractions
My thirst is clear

Highway
_hydrus

So close to me
The hungers real
Hypnotic trance
I crave a meal

Grabbing her hand
Holding it tight
Look in her eyes
Teeth want to bite

The steamy windows
Obscure the moon
I caress her neck
My lips set the mood

The kiss is deep
Twirling our tongues
Consumed retreat
We now are one

Renewed
_hydrus

My fingers need to taste everything I let go

_hydrus

The drive feels endless
I touch her knee
Slide up her dress
Slowly I tease

In this moment
I take command
Feel her moan
From my greedy hand

Rubbing
_hydrus

The ride has ended
But lust begins
Upon my steps
Our desires win

I consume her mouth
As we crash the door
Throw down our things
To paint the floor

Waited
_hydrus

Clothes come off
She takes her seat
Upon my lap
Buried in heat

Passions are fueled
And waves now flow
Spin her around
To lose control

Upon the rug
Her knees now raw
I thrust inside
To take it all

So much desire
Feeling my groans
She fueled the fire
That brought her home

Ablaze
_hydrus

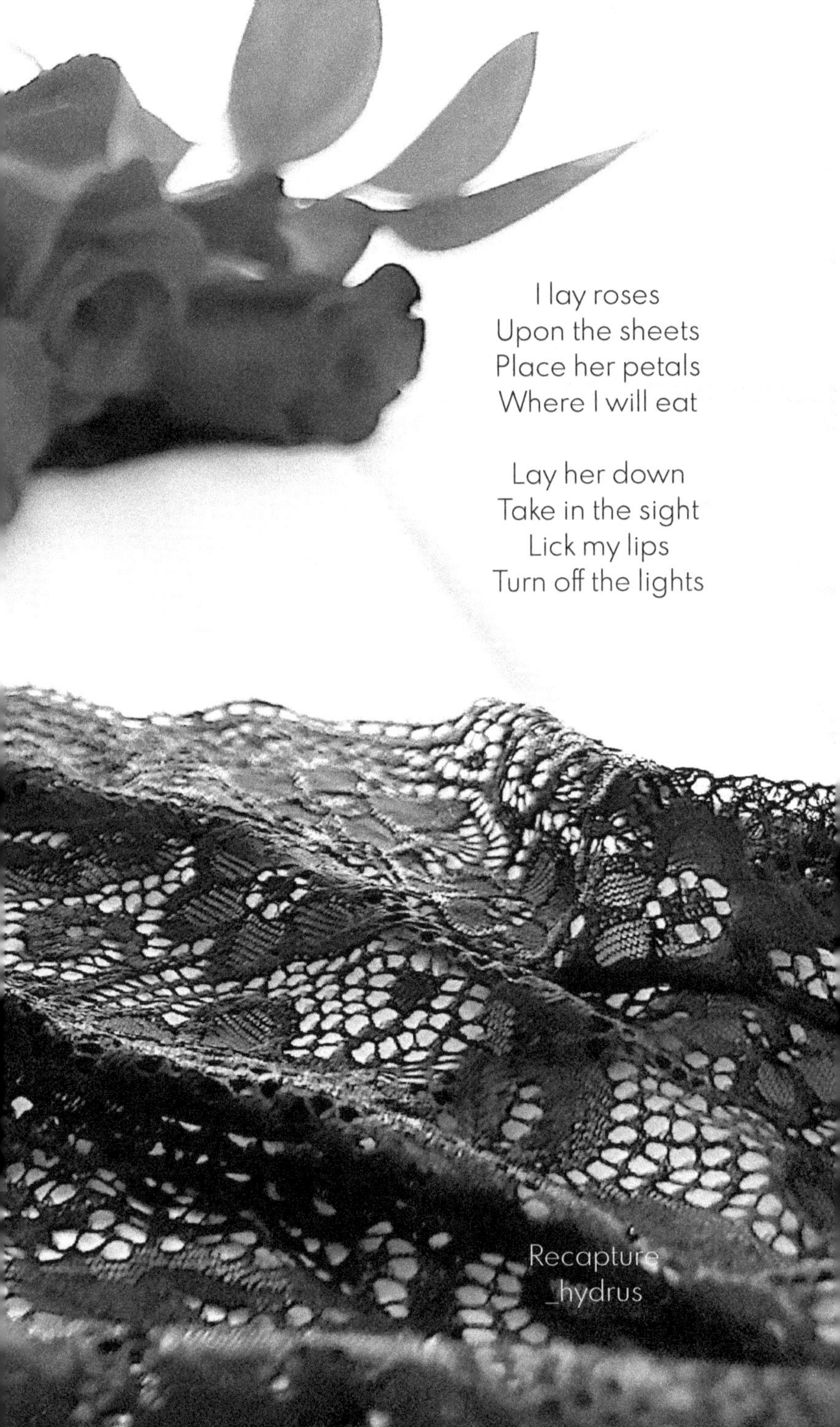

I lay roses
Upon the sheets
Place her petals
Where I will eat

Lay her down
Take in the sight
Lick my lips
Turn off the lights

Recapture
_hydrus

I take her legs
Grab her waist
Take my time
So I can taste

Swallow each finger
Bite every inch
Lick on her nipples
Before I pinch

Twist
_hydrus

Hold my head
Let me sink
Press your thighs
Watch me drink

Filling our souls
With each others' bliss
A never ending night
It's just a constant kiss

The moon now gone
And there's morning light
Rest is in my arms
Replay the night

Daybreak
_hydrus

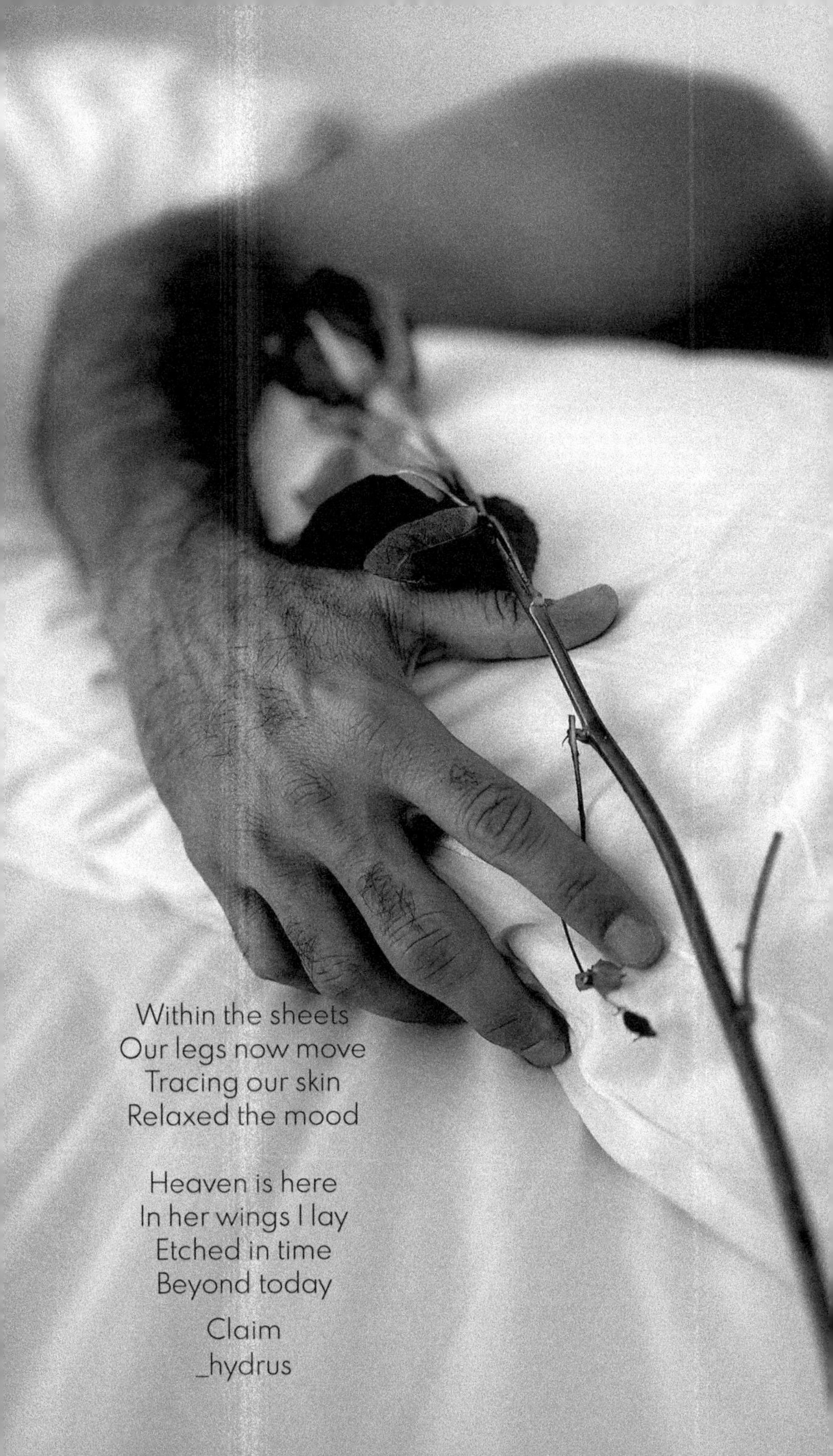

Within the sheets
Our legs now move
Tracing our skin
Relaxed the mood

Heaven is here
In her wings I lay
Etched in time
Beyond today

Claim
_hydrus

Phone now rings
For another time
She turns off the sound
Silenced the chime

Do you need to speak
It's ok I'll go
Take the call
It's her I know

Looking
_hydrus

You know the pain
I went through hell
She abused my love
Under her spell

That was long ago
You saw my fate
A tangled mess
Carved on her plate

Enchanted
_hydrus

I woke up knowing
That my heart needed to get prepared
For pain

_hydrus

She was his truth
I was just a ghost
From far away
I still felt close

Life led me here
Into his arms
Beyond my fears
Away from harm

He feels so right
With a past so wrong
Do I want this fight
I must stay strong

Doubts
_hydrus

Grabbing my things
It's time to leave
Inside my heart
Partly it grieves

I've fallen hard
It was not planned
What can I do
He's a wanted man

Consequences
_hydrus

In a daze
Just thoughts of him
The nights we spent
My endless grin

I yearn his touch
My muscles ache
Beyond a crush
Clenching I shake

Subtle the ways
He held me tight
Within his grip
It rained all night

Our selfish ways
That shook my core
I want him now
I crave him more

Pin
_hydrus

On his shoulders he bares my fate   _hydrus

Morning coffee
Black the hue
Running late
Inhale the brew

Skip the train
Hop in a ride
Restless state
Confused inside

Reach the temple
I call my job
Selling spirits
As grown men sob

Preaching stools
Listening to myths
Pouring lies
As sermons sip

Unholy vessel
Unblessed the wine
Chained existence
Where I do time

Glasses empty
I'm paid to fill
Pretending happy
That's my daily drill

Tending
_hydrus

THE MID TOWN MOB
N.Y
65
You lit every fire with just one touch   _hydrus

A mirrored backdrop
Where the bottles call
Scream in silence
As they dress the wall

Darkened oak
Enslaves the stage
Parched dried lips
Unlock their cage

In this cauldron
I play the muse
Serving inmates
Stirring their booze

On one night
I found a thief
He stole my heart
As he sadly grieved

And every day
Before last call
I reminisce
About it all

Standing alone
All I do is stare
At the place
His empty chair

Entered
_hydrus

Every pour left me empty   _hydrus

The day is quiet
Few find time for cheers
I'm lost in thought
Until I start to hear

Distant footsteps
Echo down the hall
Approach behind me
My skin starts to crawl

I spin around
To face the door
An opened space
Feeling a roar

There she stood
All dressed in black
Her sleekened mane
Primed to attack

Her claws were sharpened
Glossed in blood
Choked in pearls
Handled with gloves

Glaring in silence
I sensed the growl
My boss was here
She knew somehow

Stalked
_hydrus

Every empty glass
Is home to an empty spirit

_hydrus

Have you seen
A man in black
The one who sits
Way in the back

I need to find him
Searching in vain
He frequents here
Do you know his name

I've seen you talk
Curious for clues
You know his fame
He drinks his blues

If he comes
Bait the snare
Find me quick
Is this clear

Blair
hydrus

What have I done
Has it gone too far
I find myself
Trapped at this bar

An acute struggle
Trying to deal
In the middle
Don't know what's real

Triangle
_hydrus

You fell and I fell harder _hydrus

Fingers quiver
Lost for words
I fiercely scramble
Minds so blurred

An unwanted mess
Has found its way
Jumbling feelings
As life plays

Dialing his number
In a dark lit room
Away from eyes
Peering for my doom

He answers quickly
And can sense my fear
The devil's back
And she wants you here

Messenger
_hydrus

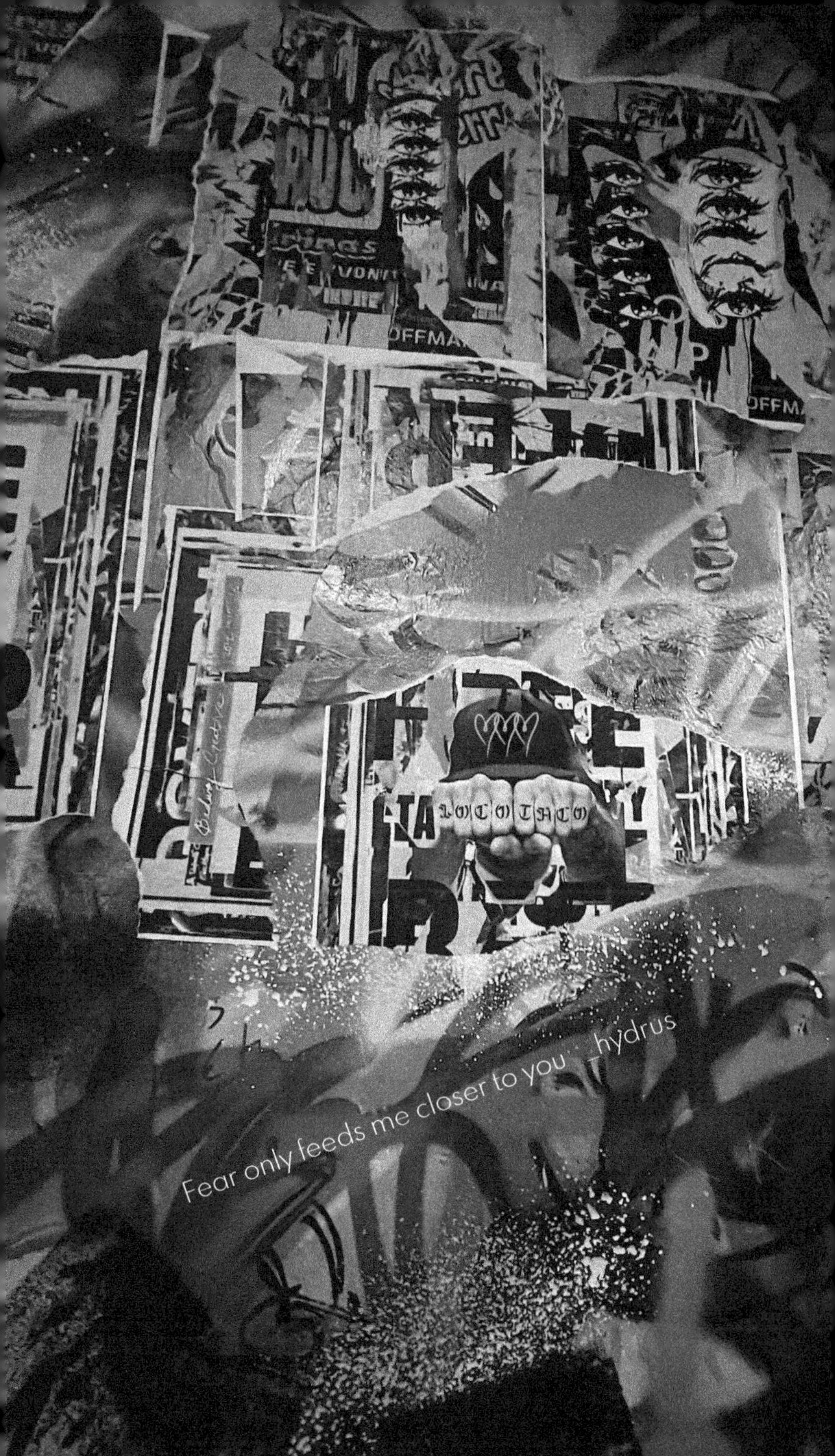
Fear only feeds me closer to you _hydrus

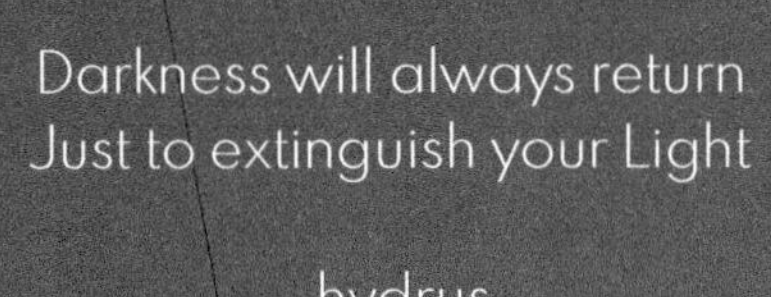

Darkness will always return
Just to extinguish your Light

_hydrus

In her voice
Trembled the seeds
The planted lies
Of my misdeeds

I let her know
There's no more there
Once it was real
Now it's all despair

We were an item
When I was lost
I had no clue
There'd be a cost

Then
_hydrus

When we met
You knew my plight
An inner struggle
A constant fight

I never ventured
Into your path
I respected you
All that we had

I never meant
To break and fall
I am to blame
My fault for all

I never thought
To love again
You brought me back
Beyond just a friend

Never Did
_hydrus

Every doubt
Decided to rest in me
Inside the shallow grave
I now call my life

_hydrus

ONE

Days have gone
Since that call
I miss his voice
I miss it all

I can't imagine
Life without him
He was my savior
When life was grim

Sent
_hydrus

Yuengli
America's Oldest Bre
BACARD
I relive every second of every drip that you are away

Another day
Standing guard
In my daze
Still feeling scarred

Ending my shift
It's much too late
Still thinking of
Our perfect date

Relived
_hydrus

As I count
Restock the wine
A burning stare
Rare at this time

I turn around
And squint my eyes
Cloaked in darkness
Sensuous disguise

Holding roses
Drenched in red
He glares right back
Tilts back his head

Showing me
Those deep brown eyes
Fires burn
I'm consumed inside

Shocked
_hydrus

Every wish starts with a goodbye   _hydrus

I had to come
See you tonight
Canceled work
Jumped on a flight

Needing to quiet
Any doubts up there
Soothing your heart
Showing you I care

Let's run away
Far from tonight
Take my hand
And let's reignite

Kiss my lips
Staking your claim
It's only us
No more games

Get Away
_hydrus

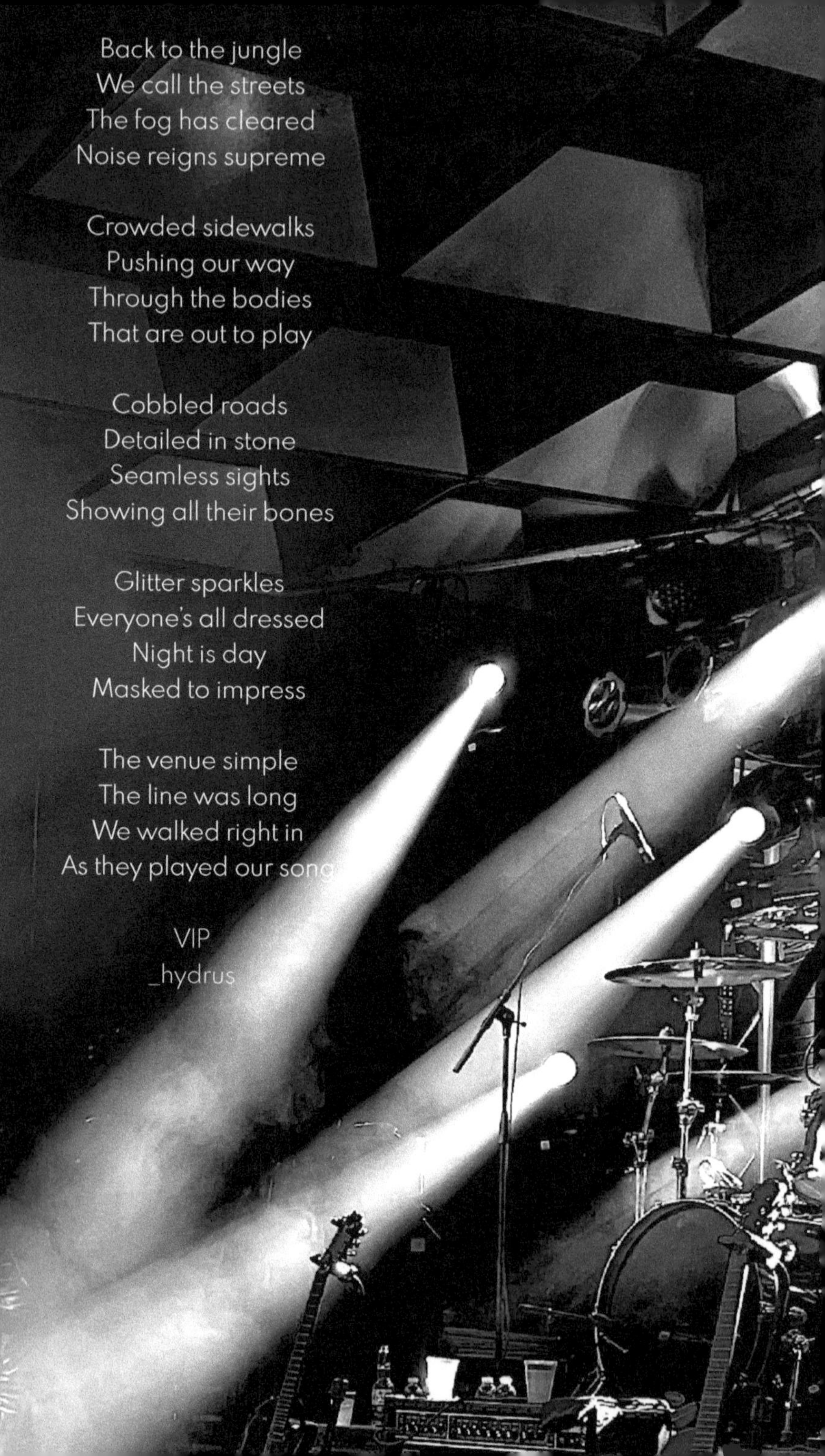

Back to the jungle
We call the streets
The fog has cleared
Noise reigns supreme

Crowded sidewalks
Pushing our way
Through the bodies
That are out to play

Cobbled roads
Detailed in stone
Seamless sights
Showing all their bones

Glitter sparkles
Everyone's all dressed
Night is day
Masked to impress

The venue simple
The line was long
We walked right in
As they played our song

VIP
_hydrus

She looked so stunning
Without a care
A radiant phoenix
Full of fire and flare

Her flames consumed me
Embraced in dance
Burning ashes
Music fueled our trance

Hands explored
Mouths reunite
Again our motions
Scorching the night

Lost in heaven
She strikes the match
Rekindled romance
Lit our path

Euphoria
_hydrus

After our dance
We then retreat
Into the dark
To a hidden seat

Champagne awaits
Chilled in a glass
She takes a sip
It doesn't last

I taste her lips
She feeds it back
Thirsty we kiss
Stroking her back

I pull her in
Up close to me
Kissing her skin
It's meant to be

Corner
_hydrus

Her fingers crawl
Straight up my leg
She feels me grow
Through pants I beg

I throb and twitch
Inside her hand
Waiter appears
She quickly stands

Abrupt
_hydrus

You exit when I enter

_hydrus

Be right back
Taking my purse
Leave him there
He sees me smirk

Eyes are fixed
As I walk away
I flip my hair
This blonde can play

Tease
_hydrus

There's no greater stage
Than being your only act

_hydrus

Stranded here
Asked for a drink
Whiskey clear
I sit and think

When suddenly
Before my eyes
It's not my Angel
A clouded sight

Remember me
She quickly quips
Made love all night
Showered with drips

You left that day
My body marked
In bed I laid
From your savage spark

Surge
_hydrus

Not every song has a memorable lyric

_hydrus

I have to go
I'm back on stage
Here's where I work
And play all day

When you leave
Don't forget to call
I'm still in town
If you want it all

Ashley
_hydrus

Obey
"MAKE ART NOT WAR"
NOT W
OBEY
Life will remind you of your bad choices   _hydrus

I can't believe
The life I lived
Parts of me
One can't forgive

I'm not the man
From long ago
A broken heart
It took its toll

Not Interested
_hydrus

Pushing back
From my seat
Race to her
I need to feast

The hungers real
I want her now
Fight the crowd
Not knowing how

Moving bodies
Out of my way
I find the door
She's locked away

It opens up
There she stands
I kiss her lips
I'm in command

Now
_hydrus

Sometimes dirty isn't dirty enough
_hydrus

Our bodies slam
Inside the stall
Pressing her back
Against the wall

Grab her pants
As the buttons fly
Rip her panties
Squeeze her thighs

Feel the cravings
As I pulse inside
Skin so tender
She begins to ride

My neck is gripped
She wraps her legs
Sensing the needs
Our flesh now begs

Thrust and moaning
As we draw a crowd
We both release
Soar above the clouds

Heaven
_hydrus

We whisk right out
Still in our high
Our timeless bliss
Touching the sky

It's my turn now
To change the chase
He awoke the beast
Back to my place

Quest
_hydrus

Every toy needs a leash _hydrus

I bring him home
Take off his clothes
He's all mine
His heart fully knows

Take my time
I'm so obsessed
Grab the ropes
As I undress

Cover his eyes
Drunk with the thrill
I tie the knots
To show my skill

I bind his arms
Then stretch his legs
Again I tease
Want him to beg

Strapped
_hydrus

I will be selfish with my hunger

_hydrus

OHHH... ALRIGHT...

The only rule is you must obey
_hydrus

Here I am
As her prey
Excitement rushes
I feel the waves

I cannot move
Bound are my hands
She takes a candle
To mark her man

The hot wax drips
On my chest
I sense the burn
My muscles tense

Then her tongue
Begins to trace
From my nipples
Up to my face

Around my lips
I feel her teeth
She starts to bite
Still dripping heat

Our mouths now meet
My hunger shows
She strokes my shaft
To feel me grow

Gates
_hydrus

She takes me in
Lapping my veins
I feel her tongue
This feels insane

Her golden hair
Adorns my chest
Feeding her mouth
I do the rest

She removes the straps
Then lets me go
I pin her arms
To begin my show

Grabbing her hips
Then roaming down
Sucking those lips
Swirling all around

Glide back up
Her nails dig in
She feels my burst
Quenched from within

Winded
_hydrus

The night is endless
Feelings are raw
We are so intense
She really has it all

I've been hurt before
Each time I climbed
Trusting every judgment
Falling every time

This feels so different
Started from the crash
Opened up my eyes
She was there at last

Passions are real
Her actions are kind
Caring and familiar
It all feels divine

Just
_hydrus

I found myself
In a state of reflection
When all I could see
Was myself in her eyes

Sewn
_hydrus

In our mess
We role and play
The bodies meet
They just obey

It doesn't stop
The spoiled sounds
Making love
Never slowing down

Under the sheets
Around the room
Drenched in our heat
Our sweet perfume

Ravaged beasts
Each were the prey
A tangled feast
Thrashed where they lay

Famished
_hydrus

She is the everlasting ember that fuels the fire

_hydrus

We find ourselves
Here again
Intertwined
Beyond just friends

So much emotion
Filling my heart
Proven devotion
Built every part

I feel so safe
When I'm with him
I am his focus
Also his sin

Where does this lead
What can we be
So many thoughts
Why he's with me

Prism
_hydrus

Rays of light
Stream across the bed
He lays on me
I caress his head

Again the sun
Greets our eyes
Lying in bed
Gazing at the sky

This pause in time
A perfect glow
Peace sets in
It's all you know

All these moments
That we reaped
Heaven's here
And it soundly sleeps

Snapshot
_hydrus

Life could not prepare me
For the trials
From which I would be hung

Labeled
_hydrus

A banging door
I awake
It takes some time
To navigate

All I hear
Is a loud distress
We both get up
I need to dress

Clamor
_hydrus

The poundings loud
I need to act
Still in my cloud
The worlds abstract

Get to the door
Who can it be
I take a look
To try and see

To my surprise
Hell awaits
She found our lair
It's at our gate

Pursuit
_hydrus

Some doors must not be opened
_hydrus

Door flies open
I see her there
We are not together
What brings her here

So much anger
With no remorse
You need to leave
I say with force

Faced
_hydrus

Thinking you
Could run away
Just move on
Forget my name

Not keep in touch
Find another prize
Leave with her
You are so wise

Venom
_hydrus

Happiness was just a tease for misery

_hydrus

She is mine
And not to blame
You are the cause
Of all my pain

Leave far from her
You must go
Far from my life
End this show

Circus
_hydrus

Keep your gem
For me she's done
I'll leave you two
You haven't won

Here is my truth
Then I will run
I carry his prize
His unborn son

Expecting
_hydrus

... To Be Continued

A FALLEND SERIES BOOK THREE

REVENDGE

_HYDRUS

AWAKEND
DARKEND
HEARTEND
ENDTHOLOGY
ENDLOVEPAIN
VALENDTINE
ENDROAD
AWAKEND
A FALLEND SERIES: BOOK ONE
_HYDRUS
Write your Soul
_hydrus

I became insane, with long intervals of horrible sanity
Edgar Allan Poe

Thank You

I want to express my profound gratitude to all of you who take the time to read my ink and share in my journey.

Thank you for all of your love and unwavering support.

I always want to touch your hearts, just as your ongoing support has profoundly touched mine.

Thank you, once again, to my incredible team!
(Cleo & Jojo)

For all of your continuous hard work. Thank you for your patience and belief in me.

You truly are the machines behind Hydrus. I am very grateful and extremely lucky to be able to work with both of you.

Thank you to all my Ravens and Hydrus Team (ARC Readers) for your continuing love and support.

You play a big part in everything I do and as always I am so humbled by your love, dedication and support.

I also want to thank you for your patience ....BrokEND took a little bit too long to arrive.

Playlist

The Death of Peace of Mind	Bad Omens
Do For Love	Black Atlass
Chills - Dark Version	Mickey Valen, Joey Myron
Hateful	Post Malone
Wasted Times	The Weeknd
Sleepless	Dutch Melrose
Never Left My Mind	PLAZA
Ghost Feelings	Avvi
BABYDOLL	Ari Abdul
Waiting For Never	Post Malone
Wicked Games	RAIGN
In My Mind	Alok, John Legend
I Wanna Be Yours	Arctic Monkeys
Sunsetz	Cigarettes After Sex
Next to You	Øneheart
Use Me (feat. 070 Shake)	PVRIS, 070 Shake
Drive You Insane	Daniel DiAngelo
Like A Villain	Bad Omens
Flawless	The Neighborhood
Fire on Fire	Sam Smith
Some Time	Daniel Di Angelo
Die For You	The Weeknd
Body	Rosenfeld
Until I found you	Stephen Sanchez
Breakfast	Dove Cameron
Come A Little Closer	Cage The Elephant
The Beach	The Neighbourhood
Something in the Orange	Summer Rios
Goodbye My Lover	James Blunt

Listen here:
bit.ly/3LNnO34

ENDVISIBLE

A collection of poems about the endless feeling of being invisible while going through the emotions and sometimes cruelties of life. Illustrated by the author's own photography, this book guides us through grief, loss and love in a dark and inspiring way typical to how Hydrus's writing helps us cope with reality.

AWAK**END**

Tarots cards, much like poems, have the ability to paint a vivid picture of what once was or what could be. They delve into the subtleties that we all carry within ourselves and the secrets that make us who we are.

AwakEND is an immersion into the world of tarot and its mysteries. Read it one way, then another, and let the words guide you into the meaning of each card.
Allow chance and curiosity to accompany you on this incredible journey and let your heart awaken to hope even after having thought everything was lost...

And who knows what secrets you might find out about yourself...

DARK**END**

Is a small look into the world I call my reality.
Through poems, photography and art, I try to capture the ups and downs of this voyage we call life, and sometimes I refer to it as just existing.
Embedded in my words are stories of emotions and feelings that range from the darkest of moments to times of having some type of hope for resolve.

Life is raw and ever-evolving, and we always seem to put ourselves last overall. Time proves to be quite relentless. I hope that we all find common ground through our everyday struggles and in the end, understand that love, although painful at times, can provide so many answers.

So the question then becomes "how can we better love ourselves?"

HEART**END**

Is about how we experience love and some of the journeys we embark on when love strikes our heart. It's about the numerous com-plex phases and ever changing stages of the purest human emotions.
It might be a first kiss, a new romance, a guilty pleasure or a sense of loss but love always helps us reach the heavens or crash down upon its shores.
Love gives even when it takes, it heals and embeds its mark and sculpts us into who we are.

"We all open our hearts and in the end this is the love we bleed."
_hydrus

ENDTHOLOGY

Is a collection of poems drawn up from experiences, thoughts, and emotions. Not everything in the world is dark, but many times we live without any light. We lose ourselves in what we consider our reality. Our souls forget what is important. At the same time, we rejoice when we regain our passion and our inner light.

We might live many lives, but which one will you always remember?

What memories will we ink?

What will have true meaning?

How will we live our END?

_hydrus

ENDLOVE ENDPAIN

A collection of poems that deal with the human struggle of being in love. The emotional roller coaster and the ups and downs that our souls take on this journey. This path is one of endless bliss but sometimes agony.

Love is always a conflict of raw emotion and trust. It is a journey we seek to take and at times we regret we do. It is a struggle between good vs. evil but mostly in ourselves.

An original collection of poetry, comprised of new works, writings, and photography. It documents the many facets of ones inner journey. It deals with our ever-changing emotions, and how the mind and heart react differently when confronted by lifes cruel ironies.

We all live inside and outside ourselves. The quiet whispers we hear and the ones we ignore. The inner voice that makes us passionate, gives us hope, or creates the monster that sharpens their teeth.

ENDroad details the winding aspects of that search for answers. It shows that we all sometimes feel the same. That we are not alone. The paths we take or the ones that take us to mold our humanity into who we are. Each one presents us with the ability for us to rediscover ourselves again.

At times we might feel lost but the truth to finding our way will always rest in our hearts.

My end does not mean I am finished
It only reveals that I am starting again.
_hydrus

What happens when life and love clash?
When desire is blinding and passion betrays?
Who do you become and where does it all END?

Welcome to WeakEND, the first book in the FallEND series.

Where we discover a man's journey to answer these questions.

"Love gave so it could take" and only his inner demons will keep him from his angels. _hydrus

About The Author

Anonymous poet, photographer and artist,
Hydrus documents through his poems the darkness and the
glimmers of life taunting us when we are in the shadows,
as well as many of the little things which make a colossal impact
on who we are.

Connect with _hydrus:

Website: www.hydruspoetry.com
Instagram: @hydruspoetry
Facebook: www.facebook.com/hydruspoetry
TikTok: @hydrus_ravens
Redbubble Merchandise:
www.redbubble.com/people/hydruspoetry/explore

How can you
Find answers
When all you
Ever loved
Is lost

_hydrus